Moe  McGlutch, He Smoked Too Much

Words & pictures by Ellen Raskin

Moe Q. McGlutch,
HE SMOKED TOO MUCH

PARENTS' MAGAZINE PRESS, NEW YORK

Copyright © 1973 by Ellen Raskin
Printed in the United States of America
All rights reserved

Library of Congress Cataloging in Publication Data
Raskin, Ellen.
  Moe Q. McGlutch, he smoked too much.

  SUMMARY: Moe Q. McGlutch paid no attention
to the advice he received from his visiting young
cousin.
  [1. Smoking—Fiction] 1. Title.
PZ7.R1817Mo   [E]   73-4383
ISBN 0-8193-0686-X   ISBN 0-8193-0687-8 (lib. bdg.)

FOR SUSIE AND JIM TOGETHER

Sunday. Little Zeke and Zack and Zelda Mae were on their way to stay with Moe Q. McGlutch.

Moe Q. McGlutch was Zelda Mae's fourth cousin twice removed, who lived in a big house near the sea.

"Now remember, Little Zeke," said his father Zack, "when we get there, don't mention the fact that Moe is so rich. And don't say he's too fat."

"What should I say?" Little Zeke asked.

"Just say 'Hello, Cousin Moe Q. McGlutch, thank you for inviting us.'"

Little Zeke repeated "Hello, Cousin Moe Q. Mc-Glutch, thank you for inviting us" ten times as he climbed the stairs and once more at the door, but Moe Q. McGlutch was not there to greet him.

Moe Q. McGlutch was in bed smoking garlic shoots, said a maid with a feather duster, and she led the zebras to their room.

So Little Zeke, Zack and Zelda Mae put on striped pajamas and went to sleep; while, in the room above, Moe Q. McGlutch blew smoke rings.

And now this horrible week begins, with a loud—a very loud—snore.

Moe Q. McGlutch snored a very loud snore. The garlic shoot fell from his mouth and burned through the bed, through the rug, through the floor.

"Sorry to drop in on you so unexpectedly," said Moe Q. McGlutch, heehawing loudly at his own joke.

"Cousin Moe Q. McGlutch, you smoke too much," said Little Zeke, "especially in bed."

"I know, I know," muttered Moe, "I know." Then he climbed over Zack, and he left the room coughing and choking. "First thing tomorrow I'm giving up smoking. Good night," gasped Moe Q. McGlutch.

Zack and Zelda Mae took turns scolding Little Zeke for being so impolite.

"But I didn't say 'rich,' and I didn't say 'fat'."

"And you didn't say 'thank you' either," said Zack, and he made Little Zeke practice his speech another ten times, and then it was Monday.

Monday. Moe Q. McGlutch didn't give up smoking. He fired the butler who emptied ashtrays instead, then took the sleepy zebras on a picnic.

Two maids served lunch; one tossed the salad; and Moe blew smoke into an old oak tree.

"Keeps the bees away," explained Moe Q. McGlutch.

Firefighters, quick to the scene, smothered the smoke, flooded the food, showered the picnic party.

"Cousin Moe Q. McGlutch, you smoke too much," cried Little Zeke, "especially in the woods."

Again Moe replied, spitting, coughing and choking: "First thing tomorrow I'm giving up smoking."

And again that night Zack and Zelda Mae scolded and made Little Zeke repeat his speech ten times.

Tuesday. Moe Q. McGlutch didn't give up smoking. He fired three serving maids instead, then took Little Zeke, Zack and Zelda Mae on a boatride.

"Now, Little Zeke," coaxed Zelda Mae, "what do you say to your cousin for this wonderful ride?"

"Cousin Moe Q. McGlutch, I see a fish-monster," said Little Zeke.

"Impossible," Moe replied. And he lighted another quack-grass stalk, and he tossed the match on the fish-monster's tail.

"Moe Q. McGlutch, you smoke too much."

"Little Zeke!" scolded Zack.

"I didn't say anything," said Little Zeke.

"The fish-monster spoke again: "Ashes and matches and quack-grass butts! I said, Moe Q. McGlutch, you smoke too much."

The frightened McGlutch began coughing and choking. "First thing tomorrow I'm giving up smoking. Really," gasped Moe Q. McGlutch.

The creature swam mostly up and down; it was dark when they reached the shore.

"Good night, Mr. Fish-monster," Little Zeke said. "Thank you for inviting us on this wonderful ride."

Wednesday. Moe Q. McGlutch didn't give up smoking. He arranged a news conference instead, and bragged about the fish-monster who knew him by name. Then he puffed away on a wormwood root as Little Zeke described the rescue to the television camera crew.

"We'll be famous," said Moe Q. McGlutch, and the zebras called all their friends long-distance to tell them about the interview.

At six o'clock Little Zeke, Zack, Zelda Mae and Moe, and everyone they knew, and a zillion folk they didn't know, turned on the news. Nothing could be seen of the zebras. Nothing but a hoof and a tail.

"Cousin Moe Q. McGlutch, you smoke too much," cried Little Zeke, "especially on television."

"Little Zeke!" scolded Zack and Zelda Mae.

And Moe Q. McGlutch, coughing and choking, said: "Some little zebras are only polite to fish."

Thursday. The zebras awoke with miserable colds. Zack made Little Zeke repeat his thank-you speech ten times. Zelda Mae made Little Zeke promise never, ever again to say that Moe Q. McGlutch smoked too much.

Moe Q. McGlutch, still smoking, fired the maid who dusted the television sets, then served hot soup to the zebras in bed.

"Now, Little Zeke," coaxed Zelda Mae, "what do you say to your good cousin?"

Little Zeke studied the ashes floating in his okra soup and said, "I'm not hungry."

Friday. Moe Q. McGlutch, smoking stinkweeds, fired the cook, then took the zebras to the zoo.

"Now, Little Zeke," coaxed Zelda Mae, "what do you say to your kind cousin Moe for those four—I mean three—balloons?"

"Moe Q. McGlutch, I love you so much."

"Why, Little Zeke, what a nice thing to say," said a very surprised Zack; but Little Zeke, down to his last balloon, had not spoken a single word.

"Moe Q. McGlutch, I love you so much," repeated the fire-breathing, smoke-eating dragon.

"Everybody everywhere loves Moe Q. McGlutch," said Moe Q. McGlutch. He heehawed loudly, burned a hole in Zack's sweater, tossed a butt into Zelda Mae's bag, and blew smoke into the chauffeur's eyes.

Then Little Zeke shouted just as loud as he could:
"Cousin Moe Q. McGlutch, you smoke too much!"
This time Zack didn't scold. Neither did Zelda Mae.

Saturday. Little Zeke, Zack and Zelda Mae, in maids' disguise, followed the fired chauffeur out the door.

The zebras knew their cousin would beg them to stay, but they didn't dare spend another day with the smoke-ring-blowing, stinkweed-smoking, dangerous Moe Q. McGlutch.

"Good-by, Cousin Moe Q. McGlutch," Little Zeke called back. "Thank you for inviting us."

"Shush, Little Zeke," scolded Zack and Zelda Mae.

They were too far away to see the dragon. They were too far off to hear Moe, coughing and choking, say: "First thing tomorrow I'm giving up smoking."

Saturday. One week later the dragon, much fatter and blowing smoke rings, was recaptured. Clutched in his claw was a carton that read:

Stinkweed

SMOKING IS DANGEROUS TO YOUR HEALTH

I know, I know; so I leave my house, my car and all my wealth to wise Little Zeke. Good-bye.
(signed) *Moe Q. McGlutch*

Rich Little Zeke rehired the fired servants, threw away the ashtrays and invited his mother and father to live with him forever in the big house near the sea.

And ten times each day, Monday through Friday; five times each Saturday and once more on Sundays, Little Zeke made Zack and Zelda Mae say:

Poor Moe Q. McGlutch, he smoked too much.

Poor Moe Q. McGlutch, he smoked too much.

Poor Moe Q. McGlutch, he smoked too much.

Poor Moe Q. McGlutch, he smoked too much.

Poor Moe Q. McGlutch, he smoked too much.